ALL THE LIGHT WE CANNOT SEE

SIDEKICK

to the novel

by

Dave Eagle

Published by

WeLoveNovels

II

Disclaimer: This publication is an unofficial Sidekick to *All the Light We Cannot See* and does not contain the novel. It is designed for fiction enthusiasts who are reading the novel, or have just finished. Order a copy of the novel *All the Light We Cannot See* on Amazon.

WeLoveNovels maintains an independent voice in delivering critical analysis and commentary; we are not affiliated with or endorsed by the publisher or author of *All the Light We Cannot See*.

Questions? Ideas? Comments?

Email founders@welovenovels.com.

We are listening!

IV

Table of Contents

INTRODUCTION 7

EXPLORING THE AUTHOR'S FICTIONAL WORLD 11

CHAPTER ANALYSIS & DISCUSSION 15

IMAGINING ALTERNATE ENDINGS 55

THEMES & SYMBOLS YOU MAY HAVE MISSED 57

A CLOSER LOOK: WERNER 61

IF YOU LOVED THIS NOVEL... 65

POSSIBLE STORYLINES FOR A SEQUEL 67

IN THE FINAL ANALYSIS... 69

ABOUT THE AUTHOR OF THIS SIDEKICK 73

VI

Introduction

Anthony Doerr may not be a household name, but that isn't due to lack of talent. To be fair, he's pretty well acclaimed in the literary world—he's won scores of awards, including a Guggenheim fellowship—and *All the Light We Cannot See* is shaping up to be his breakout novel. It's up for the National Book Award and is also a New York Times bestseller, the kind of intersection of success that most authors can only dream of. It's easy to see why: in *All the Light We Cannot See,* it doesn't take long before Doerr's unique approach to form and content hooks you and reels you in.

For this novel, Doerr's writing in strictly a postmodern aesthetic. Postmodern literature is noted for the way it breaks with traditional storytelling approaches: its hallmarks are odd punctuation, fractured timelines, fragmented sentence construction, paradox, and any other element that pushes the boundaries of the straight, linear narrative. The postmodern movement itself developed after—and as a reaction to—World War II, a conflict so gruesome and rule-breaking that it left the world too weary to explain what the hell just happened. Doerr's decision to employ several of these techniques, and to allow the structure of his novel to add to the tension, is the badge of a smart writer, capable of getting at some very big ideas in his or her work. On this front, Doerr does not disappoint.

How to Get the Most out of this Sidekick

The next two sections of this Sidekick— *Exploring the Author's Fictional World* and *Chapter Analysis & Discussion*—will be most useful <u>while</u> you are reading the novel. All subsequent sections—from *Imagining Alternate Endings* all the way through to *Possible Storylines for a Sequel*—are designed to be read <u>after</u> you have finished the novel.

If you have not yet done so, you may order a copy of the novel *All the Light We Cannot See* on Amazon. Neither I nor WeLoveNovels has any affiliation with the publisher or author of *All the Light We Cannot See*. No matter where you are in your reading of the book, with this Sidekick you will get an independent voice with insightful critical analysis and commentary.

All the Light We Cannot See
A Sidekick to the Anthony Doerr Novel

Exploring the Author's Fictional World

The world that Doerr has committed to paper is one that is very familiar to us. In 2014, seventy years after D-Day, the world still strives to process, understand, and (maybe) learn a few things from World War II. It's been examined from nearly every possible angle: historical texts and analyses, newsreel footage, newspaper accounts, photos, and film from the front lines and concentration camps. This is a world that writers, filmmakers, musicians—all artists, really—have attempted to make sense of. Doerr uses the structure of his novel, from the way he plots out the action to the tempo of each section, to create tensions that might not be there in a straight, historical accounting of the story.

He also gives us two unique perspectives on World War II. Doerr's French protagonist is Marie-Laure, whose blindness lets us "see" the horrors of occupied France in a totally new way. In order to get inside Marie-Laure's head, Doerr mixes and matches sensory descriptions—amping up smells and sounds—immersing the reader in her experience. The main German character, a young boy named Werner Pfennig, is not a typical portrayal of the "enemy." Werner is neither a vocal objector nor a conspicuous supporter of the Nazi regime under which he lives and eventually serves. He's somewhere in between, trying to escape his unhappy childhood by using the machinery of Germany to pursue his dream of a scientific education. From that perspective, we get a much different, more sympathetic, look at the Germans who fought in the War than we're used to.

All the Light We Cannot See
A Sidekick to the Anthony Doerr Novel

Chapter Analysis & Discussion

Part Zero

What's important about Part Zero is not so much what happens over the course of its sixteen pages. Part Zero exists so that Anthony Doerr can tell us how to read his book; it's a kind of literary map to navigate through his world. The name itself is peculiar, because what does it mean to be the zeroth part of a book? Why not call it a Prologue or some other more conventional term? The novel's epigraph gives us a germ of information about Saint-Malo, a historic walled city in France that had been bombed to smithereens in August of 1944. And then, right away, the narrative places us in that very city on the eve of its destruction. We're at Ground Zero.

If you skimmed through the Table of Contents before reading—some of them, like this one, can be quite informative—you'll have noticed a couple of peculiar things apart from Part Zero. First, there are an astounding 178 chapters in the novel, split into 14 parts. Second, the story is *not* told entirely in chronological order, and the novel opens at what appears to be the moment just before the story reaches its climax. Doerr plants us in the action ahead of time, but only in brief flashes. Each scene comes into focus and then disappears quickly, little explosions of scene-setting, a device which foreshadows the actual bombing that we already know will happen. We're introduced to the novel's two main characters as each prepares for the coming airstrike. Marie-Laure, sixteen years old and blind, is hiding under a bed, clutching a small stone—the size of a pigeon's egg, we're told—to her chest. Werner Pfennig is in the cellar of an old hotel, thinking of his childhood. Having introduced us to them at this incredibly tense moment, Doerr lets the bombs drop and the anti-aircraft shells fly, and then closes Part Zero by literally fading to black. The one light bulb in the cellar where Werner is goes out, leaving him—and us—in darkness. All that's left is the light we cannot see.

Part One

After giving us our brief and frantic introduction to the characters and setting of *All the Light We Cannot See*, Doerr goes back in time and slows down considerably. We meet Marie-Laure when she still has sight—barely. She is touring the National Museum of Natural History in Paris, where her father works. There she learns about a valuable diamond the museum has hidden behind thirteen doors: the Sea of Flames, a stone the size of a pigeon's egg that is said to be cursed (whoever holds the diamond is safe from harm or death, but everyone else in their life falls victim to some tragedy). When Marie-Laure's sight goes for good, her father builds a scale-model replica of their neighborhood so she can learn to navigate it by herself. We then meet Werner Pfennig, who lives with his sister Jutta in a German orphanage and has a gift for working with electronics, particularly radios. It's unclear how the paths of these two will cross, if at all, but clearly Doerr has some kind of link in mind.

Both have hard-luck stories: Marie-Laure has lost her mother and her sight—for her, the light has nearly gone out, both figuratively and literally. Werner has no parents and, it seems, no real future: under Nazi rule, all boys in the town where he lives must go to work in the pitch black of the mines at the age of fifteen. Doerr also subtly ties the two characters together through the importance of sound in their worlds. Many of the descriptions that we get of Marie-Laure's world have to do with her remaining senses, and sound is a huge part of her awareness of her surroundings. Meanwhile, Werner's passion for radio means that he is often scanning shortwave frequencies and listening to foreign broadcasts as a way of orienting himself within a larger world. Of particular interest to him and his sister is a beautifully written French science program— its technical information fascinates Werner, but it's the poetic tone of the words and the sound of the narrator's voice that strike a chord with Jutta.

As Part One concludes and World War II approaches, we watch both Marie-Laure and Werner as their personal trajectories seemingly pass each other: Marie-Laure loses nearly everything as she and her father flee Paris ahead of the German airstrikes (with the cursed *Sea of Flames*, or its replica, in their possession); Werner gains the opportunity of his dreams as his aptitude for electronics is rewarded with a state-sponsored education to follow his passion (and avoid the mines). His reputation as a whiz with radios lands him in the posh housing of a German officer who needs a repair.

When Werner is first asked after at the orphanage, he's convinced he and Jutta have been found out: that the Nazis know they've been listening to foreign broadcasts. Though he is relieved this isn't the case, and welcomes the change in his fortunes this episode brings, he still smashes the radio that he and his sister spent so many nights escaping with. Perhaps it's for her own safety, or maybe he's just letting go of his idealistic youth. Werner isn't much a fan of the strict living conditions enforced by his government, but he abandons any reservations he may have to make the most of the opportunity that's been given him.

All the Light We Cannot See
A Sidekick to the Anthony Doerr Novel

Part Two

Doerr takes another trip forward, back to August 1944, and puts us right in the middle of the attack on Saint-Malo. Again, we catch only brief glimpses of what happens, but the descriptions are so vivid and unsettling that brief is all we need. Werner is trapped under the rubble of what used to be a hotel. He is disoriented, injured, and can hear only a roar in his ears. Marie-Laure can feel and hear fire advancing on her great uncle's house, and she makes her way down to the cellar for safety. Part Two ends as quickly as it began, and with no less uncertainty.

The way Doerr plays with time is instrumental in creating higher stakes for the reader. Were this all told in a straightforward chronology, we might not be as involved or invested in the characters. But because the narrative flashes back and forth, each of these small revelations feeds the drama that came before and after it. As we read Part One, we get to know the characters a little, and knowing that something awful is going to happen to them colors the way we perceive every event in their lives. It only took ten or so pages for Doerr to seriously raise the stakes of the book, adding more weight to the next part as we head back to 1940 again.

Part Three

We pick up where we left off at the end of Part One, with Marie-Laure and her father, Daniel, fleeing Paris. Daniel hopes to deliver the *Sea of Flames* to a colleague (and receive the meal and shelter that will no doubt follow). The pair arrives to find their destination in flames, its owners long since gone. They press on to Saint-Malo, where Daniel's uncle, Etienne, has a house. Marie-Laure has never met her great uncle, and the only thing she knows about him is that he was never the same after coming back from World War I—the experience had driven him crazy. Or rather, 76% crazy, as Daniel describes it. He sees things that aren't there, and he hasn't left the house in twenty years. Marie-Laure is both excited and confused about their stay in Saint-Malo: she wants very much to explore the city and go to the ocean, which she has read about in her Jules Verne books, but her father won't let her out of the house. Instead, he always promises a trip in some ill-defined future. Until they fled, Marie-Laure's world was, by necessity, one of routine and logic. Now she's stuck in a strange house with a strange great uncle and with no clear timetable for a return home (to say nothing of just going outside).

As Marie-Laure's existence slips further from her control, Werner becomes serious about steering his future toward his goals. Jutta doesn't take the news lightly when Werner tells her that he's been offered what he sees as a great opportunity. Her anger at him comes off as petty jealousy at first—younger sister mad at her older brother for abandoning her—but when they speak, we learn there is more to her objection. Having used their radio to listen to the news and commentary coming from around the world, she's heard an opposing view to the Nazi story of Aryan supremacy.

"Broadcasts from Paris," she tells him, "They'd say we were devils. That we were committing atrocities."

Here we see the power of the media and propaganda, which is starting to develop as a theme in this novel. The second part of the epigraph to the book is a quote from Joseph

Goebbels, who was Hitler's close associate and Minister of Propaganda. "It would not have been possible for us to take power or to use it in the ways we have without the radio." Goebbels's quote shines a light on the ease with which government can sway its people when it controls the flow of information. Werner's personal struggle mirrors the state of most of Germany following the First World War. The whole country was in depression, psychically and financially, following the Treaty of Versailles. The rise of Adolf Hitler and his Nazi party brought prosperity and national pride back to Germany. Given Werner's desperation to rise above his meager beginnings, we can understand why he makes the choices he does; it's hard not to think of the rest of Germany as millions of individuals in a similar situation, able to look past certain things because they're personally doing better and the news on the radio tells them what they want to hear. Jutta's questioning of the accepted story shines as an example of why dictatorships must restrict access to outside sources of information.

Of course, propaganda is just an institutional version of the type of myth and fable that most cultures are steeped in. Are the stories the Nazi-sanctioned media peddles any more or less logical than the museum where Daniel LeBlanc works keeping a diamond hidden away under lock and key because of a centuries-old curse? As Part Three moves on, this jewel becomes increasingly important. The government of France is going to great lengths to protect it. Its value is based in its history—the curse, the story—and we're introduced to Sergeant Major Reinhold von Rumpel, who's been tasked with finding the diamond. Meanwhile, Daniel LeBlanc has been arrested by the Germans after a neighbor sees him pacing the streets of Saint-Malo (measuring distances for the scale model he's building for Marie-Laure to help her learn the area) and deems his behavior suspicious—and profitable.

In the meantime, Marie-Laure develops a bond with her great uncle, whom she finds to be quite sane—at least during the short periods of time he leaves his room or allows visitors in. Etienne and Marie-Laure are both trapped in the house, for different reasons, and they take great comfort in each other as they read from Charles Darwin's travel and science memoir, *The Voyage of the Beagle.* With their imaginations and a flying couch, the two fly across the globe, visiting all the spots Darwin saw. And here, again, we see the tenuous links between Marie-Laure and Werner growing stronger. They are each on some kind of personal journey as they grow beyond the bounds of their previous existences. Marie-Laure must step outside the logic and predictability of her life in Paris—such things no longer hold much sway in her new reality—and rely on flights of fancy to sustain her through an uncertain time. She learns of the radio transmitter that her great uncle built to send comforting sounds out to his brother—her grandfather. As it happens, Etienne's been broadcasting recordings of his brother's voice: it's the very same science show that instilled wonder in Jutta and enough fear in Werner that he smashed the radio to prevent his sister from hearing it again. It becomes clear now that smashing the radio had great symbolic significance in Werner's mind. There was magic and danger in the voices he listened to, and only by shutting them out could he move forward, away from what he felt was the trap of his life. But the radio also held a place of significance in his bond with Jutta; it literally kept them close as they both listened to it. In smashing the radio, Werner took something from his sister, and as his eyes begin to open to the reality of Nazi Germany, he thinks of how she would not approve of the things he's witnessed.

Part Four

We are back at August 8, 1944, just after the bombing of Saint-Malo. Doerr continues to paint a scene of destruction that is steeped as much in emotion as it is in imagery. We are now seventy years past the events of this day during World War II, a long enough time that we tend to forget the modernity of this particular war. Doerr's descriptions bring us right into it, though, as we read about city buildings burning in passages that could very well have come right out of 9/11: "From afar, the smoke appears strangely solid, as though carved from luminous wood. All along its perimeter, sparks rise and ash falls and administrative documents flutter: utility plans, purchase orders, tax records." Whether or not these details are true to the scene in question is irrelevant. Doerr is purposely trading in language that we'll understand, words that will put us right in the center of the destruction. These scenes are all the more palpable since we have a common reference point to dwell on.

For this third visit back to the day when Saint-Malo was destroyed, we get more glimpses into the future of this story that's slowly unfolding, the story of the ten years leading to this moment. Sergeant Major von Rumpel is still searching for the diamond, and he knows that it's in the house where Marie-Laure is hiding. Werner, whose father died in a mine, and who felt trapped by the misfortunes of his life, now finds himself trapped for real, underground and injured. He is in complete darkness except for the moments when his fellow soldier (and former classmate) Volkheimer turns on a flashlight to assess the situation. When the light is off, they are in total darkness, which Werner soon learns isn't darkness after all. "Even total darkness is not quite darkness" once the eyes adjust, but Werner is never fully able to acclimate. Volkheimer continues turning on his light, illuminating his surroundings, and then turning it off, leaving them in all the light they cannot see. In his mind, Werner catalogs all their possessions, trying to formulate a way out of the cellar. He can only come up with a plan involving Volkheimer's rifle and five bullets, more than enough to put him,

Volkheimer, and the injured Bernd out of their misery.

Part Four closes on a suspenseful note: Sergeant Major Von Rumpel is in Saint-Malo, and he's got his eye on Etienne's house. He is in great pain, as "a black vine has grown branches through his legs and arms" and it's only a matter of time before it "chokes off his heart." Being terminally ill seems to have made finding the *Sea of Flames* a more personal quest; it appears Von Rumpel has bought into its legend. Marie-Laure, alone in her great uncle's house, is aware that someone has just entered the premises, thanks to a trip wire Etienne set up.

Part Five

SPOILER ALERT

This is a good moment to pause and reflect on the title of the book. We could spend an entire Sidekick unpacking the title alone—*All the Light We Cannot See* is wonderfully evocative, but of what? There's the obvious reference to Marie-Laure's blindness; the daylight that Werner can't see while trapped under the hotel; the voice of Marie-Laure's grandfather reading the words of her great-uncle, heard by Werner and Jutta over the airwaves: *Open your eyes, and see what you can with them before they close forever.* But there's also the influence of language: when we say we have "seen the light," we're speaking about having a new or greater level of understanding of something. What does it mean, then, to speak about the light you cannot see? We've seen how Doerr touched on the concepts of storytelling and its influence on culture, whether through propaganda or through legend. But what happens when our personal narratives—the stories we tell ourselves—prevent us from seeing the light?

For Werner, he spent his childhood stuck in a place he never wanted to be, doomed to work in a job he never wanted to do. He convinced himself that having the state sponsor him at an elite school was the right thing for his future, and he chose to look the other way when confronted with what was behind it. The reality of the Nazi regime forces its way into Werner's conscience—he begins to see the instructors for who they are as they have the boys torture a prisoner and then leave the corpse on display for a few weeks. He watches the bullying against his friend Frederick escalate to disturbing heights, sanctioned and encouraged by his teacher, Bastian. Through all of this, and in the shame he feels for choosing this life over one with his sister, Werner frequently breaks from reality and has visions of himself back home. He's seeing the dreaded place he wanted so desperately to leave in an entirely different light. When Frederick disappears one day and it's clear he's been beaten—possibly to death—Werner has seen too much. In some ways, Werner's experience parallels that of Marie-Laure with her scale models. She studies her world in miniature to gain a better understanding of the world around her. Similarly, Werner needs to see the horrors of his country in miniature before he can fully understand his own environment. It's one thing to hear a distant broadcast about atrocities perpetrated in service to the Reich; it's another to know your friend has been savagely beaten, ostensibly for the same reason. Despite all his success working with Dr. Hauptmann—they've been able to repeatedly triangulate locations using transmitters and receivers—Werner asks his mentor to let him go home. It does not go well, to say the least: Hauptmann declares that Werner is older than he claimed and sends him off to the front lines.

Marie-Laure, on the other hand, exists in a state somewhere between true happiness and utter depression. Her father leaves Saint-Malo, called away by the Museum (or perhaps not—it isn't clear whether he was set up by his neighbor), and is arrested before he reaches Paris. Etienne retreats back into his room in depression and fear. Madame Manec defies

Daniel's wishes and takes Marie-Laure out of the house and, finally, to the ocean. The language that Doerr uses to describe her first meeting with the sea is perfectly crafted, landing on all the senses that become heightened with the loss of sight. He describes her as standing in "a portal of sound larger than anything she has ever imagined," feeling the "thousand tiny spines of raindrops melt onto her cheeks." How many of us with sight take in a view of the ocean and tune out all these things, or at least push them to the background? This is the light that Marie-Laure sees. As she meets more people in the town, her life seems to spring into purpose. She accompanies Mme. Manec around town: they bring food to Crazy Harold Bazin, disfigured and alone after World War I, and they exchange plans with other women for random acts of mischief to perpetrate on their occupiers. These activities are a source of tension between Etienne and Mme. Manec; he does not want to risk arousing suspicion, while she wants to up the stakes, even asking Etienne to broadcast codes for her group with his transmitter. Marie-Laure is less affected by this tension than she might have been when she was locked in the house; she feels a new sense of freedom. Harold Bazin gives her his key to a secret grotto built into the city ramparts that block out the sea. Inside is a protected natural habitat filled with sea creatures. Marie-Laure is seeing more than she ever has in her life. When Mme. Manec dies of pneumonia at the end of Part Five, yet another light in Marie-Laure's life is snuffed out.

Part Six

We return again to 1944. Marie-Laure escapes to the attic through a hidden door Etienne installed in the wardrobe that obstructs the real door up to the attic. Von Rumpel is in the house and begins slowly, though not steadily, making his way through the rooms. Marie-Laure recognizes his odd gait, which tells us that he's been there at least once before. This is another one of those puzzle pieces that Doerr is so good at placing: we're reading a scene that happens chronologically after a previous visit, but we haven't yet read about that visit. This helps to create more tension when the story goes back to 1942—we'll read with worry knowing that at any moment Nazis could show up at Etienne's door and upset whatever fragile balance remains. Not coincidentally, this was the fear that was on every French person's mind during the occupation, and so it helps the reader get a greater level of empathy for the characters in the novel. Right now, though, in the narrative, Marie-Laure has hidden herself away, six stories up in the air, in an attic filled with radio equipment. In the same town, Werner is trapped underground with Volkheimer and the now-dead Bernd. He's rounded up what materials he could find and is trying to fix the radios that are his and his friend's only chance for survival. And so we end this brief trip back to 1944 with an image of Marie-Laure perched high above the streets and Werner trapped below them, both armed with transmitters and receivers, and the space between them suddenly like the conduit through which their stories will cross.

Part Seven

Thankfully, the depression that Etienne experiences in the wake of Mme. Manec's death gives way to resolve. No longer content to sulk and hide away, Etienne enlists the help of Marie-Laure to honor Mme. Manec's request. They begin broadcasting strings of numbers—their meaning and recipients unknown—which Marie-Laure gets from the local bakery, hidden inside loaves of bread. Etienne starts playing music along with his recitations of codes, and he begins to really enjoy his life. One evening, the thrill of it all—the secrecy, the subversion—gets the best of him, and after reading the numbers he lets the music and the transmitter go a little longer while he dances with Marie-Laure. After this happens, the narration tells us that "the bony figure of Death" is approaching their house on horseback on the streets below. Etienne thinks to himself, "Pass us by, Horseman. Pass this house by." It sounds like Etienne is at the moment 76% crazy and seeing things that aren't there. But we know that Von Rumpel could show up at any point, and it suddenly doesn't seem so crazy that there might be someone patrolling the streets below.

While Marie-Laure and Etienne broadcast codes to resistance fighters, Werner is using his radio triangulation method to locate citizens broadcasting such codes. And just as Etienne reminds himself that his dance with his grand-niece is what he's fighting for, Werner has a similar moment of lightness watching a young girl on a swing at a playground. Her eyes remind him of Jutta's, and he thinks to himself, "This is life...this is why we live, to play like this on a day when winter is finally releasing its grip." But the worry that Etienne carries over having left the mic open too long is nothing compared to the horror Werner feels at seeing the girl from the swings dead, killed by his fellow soldier. It was an accident—a bad decision with terrible consequences—but Werner remains haunted by the image of the girl. And we can't help but think of the danger Etienne and Marie-Laure may be in when Werner is thinking things like, "They raise the antenna too high, broadcast for too many minutes, assume the world offers safety and rationality when of course it does not."

But if the world does not offer rationality, what are we to make of Von Rumpel, travelling all over Europe in search of a diamond he believes has magical powers and will cure his cancer?

Part Eight

Marie-Laure is beginning to buy into the diamond's power herself—or, at least, she's trying to talk herself out of doing so. Part Eight opens with Marie-Laure hiding in the attic from Von Rumpel, who is straggling and groaning along and every so often saying aloud, "The house is missing, where are you house?" She wants desperately to eat something, but her father's voice echoes in her head, telling her not to make any noise. She argues internally with this projection of her father, who is telling her the diamond will protect her. But Marie-Laure has, in some ways, outgrown her father, and she goes ahead and opens a can of beans using a knife, cleverly striking it with a brick in time with the rhythm of the falling bombs. She puts herself in further danger by leaving the attic and getting some water, but she's in survival mode.

Meanwhile, Werner has given up. He tinkers with radio parts and scans frequencies until he depletes the battery. Werner figures they have enough juice in the backup battery to get either one day's worth of light or one day's worth of radio use. He then notes the rifle would not require anything further to work. He's given up. He and Volkheimer lack the energy and oxygen to do anything but sit back and wait to die. He continues searching the airwaves to find someone broadcasting, and finds Marie-Laure reading from *20,000 Leagues Under the Sea*, punctuating sentences by whispering into the microphone that she's in danger. Again, Werner's thoughts go to Jutta and it's unclear who he's thinking of when we read: *"Do something. Save her."*

Part Nine

Up until this point, the story has been revealed over the course of two parallel narratives: the first, a series of vignettes, flashes of scenes over the course of a bit more than a day; the other, a slowly unfolding story of the ten years leading up to the day of the bombing. The rhythm of the novel was established early and sustained for roughly 400 pages, and that's all about to change. Part Nine begins in May 1944, just three months before the destruction of Saint-Malo. Werner's team has been sent to the Brittany area of France to search for illegal broadcasts and dispose of those transmitting (Etienne and Marie-Laure). No one else is awake when Werner finally finds them, and there is something in Etienne's voice and delivery, coupled with the music, that transports him back to those nights he and Jutta listened to Etienne's brother read his words. Werner later denies having heard any broadcasts—we don't know whether he does so as an act of tenderness for this man whose radio scripts inspired him so many years ago, or because he truly thinks they weren't broadcasting codes to help resistance fighters. No matter, though; Werner finds the exact house with the antenna so he can meet the man behind the mic. Before he can knock, Marie-Laure exits the house. Werner silently follows her, seemingly smitten.

On her way back to Etienne's, she's confronted by Von Rumpel, though Doerr doesn't let us in on that right away. The narration takes on Marie-Laure's point of view, and thus we don't get a look at the man speaking. Even though we've been expecting Von Rumpel, Doerr purposely misleads us, putting us at the same disadvantage Marie-Laure is at. Von Rumpel speaks French, but she can tell he's German, which could lead us to think he's Werner. At first, his dialogue seems pleasant enough, but his questions are never-ending. He calls her on the inconsistencies in her answers and speaks of her father in a menacing way. Von Rumpel's identity is confirmed by the "one-pause-two" of his footsteps—the way Marie-Laure recognized him earlier in the book (but later in the action), when he showed up looking for the *Sea of Flames*. Von

Rumpel presses her to tell him what her father may have left her, and she finally loses her cool with him, though what she screams seems directed at her father: "He left me *nothing*. Nothing! Just a dumb model of this town and a broken promise." This incident leads Etienne to confine Marie-Laure to the house, and he takes on the task of retrieving the codes from the bakery. He leaves the house for the first time in twenty-four years and tells Marie-Laure that she is "the best thing that has ever come into my life."

Werner, it seems, feels similarly. He cannot stop thinking of Marie-Laure, and he continues to pretend he never heard Etienne's broadcast, planning to keep it a secret. As Part Nine comes to a close, we've come full circle. We find out that Etienne has been arrested, explaining his absence during the bombing. But the section closes the same way the book opens: it's August 7, 1944, and leaflets are raining from the sky.

Part Ten

SPOILER ALERT

It is four days after the bombing of Saint-Malo. Von Rumpel is still slowly dying in Etienne's house, taking it apart, looking for the diamond. Marie-Laure is still upstairs, hidden away in the attic with one remaining can of unknown food. Werner and Volkheimer lie under the Hotel of Bees, waiting for the inevitable. When Marie-Laure decides she's had enough, she tries to speed things up. She spins Debussy's "Claire de Lune" up on the record player, turns the volume all the way up, and broadcasts. Someone will find her, or Von Rumpel will hear her: either way, she's ending the waiting game. The sounds of "Claire de Lune"—and if you're not familiar with the title, trust that you know the tune, and believe me that it is that beautiful—stir Volkheimer to abandon his acceptance of what's to come and arrive at a decision. He's going to try and blow his way out with a grenade. He'll clear out an opening, or the grenade will kill both him and Werner: either way, he's ending the waiting game.

Volkheimer and Werner make it out; Von Rumpel hears the music coming from upstairs. Werner and Von Rumpel converge on the sixth floor of Etienne's house while Marie-Laure waits on the other side of wardrobe, knife in hand. Very quickly, she realizes that there are two men there. She hears a scuffle and then a gunshot. Werner has shot Von Rumpel and rescues Marie-Laure. There seems to be an instant connection between them; the conversation is easy, light. Werner walks through his brief moments with Marie-Laure there-but-not-there, wholly engrossed in her and also wistful as he wishes it could last forever. They spend the night in Etienne's cellar, waiting for the ceasefire to begin. When the bombs stop dropping and the world outside falls silent, Werner helps Marie-Laure get to safety, then leaves her. Their parting is quick and understated. Soon, Marie-Laure is reunited with Etienne, and Werner is dead, having stepped on a landmine left behind by German soldiers.

All the Light We Cannot See
A Sidekick to the Anthony Doerr Novel

Parts Eleven, Twelve, and Thirteen

Each of these three parts acts as a distinct epilogue to the story. Any one of them on its own would have been a satisfying ending, but together they add a deeper meaning to the story than a simple "Where are they now?" section. Part Eleven takes us through 1945 and the aftermath of the war. Etienne and Marie-Laure have gone to live in the apartment in France where Marie-Laure grew up. We finally rejoin Jutta, sent to work first in factories, then doing war cleanup. Russian soldiers find her and her fellow workers and systematically rape them.

In Part Twelve, Werner's spirit seems to float from place to place as we check back in with everyone thirty years later, in 1974. We start with Volkheimer, a TV antenna repairmen (inspired by Werner?) who receives a piece of mail from a veterans' organization asking for his help in identifying the owner of some items recovered. He recognizes Werner's notebook in one of the pictures they sent. Next, we see Jutta in her home. She's forty-three, married, and a schoolteacher. Volkheimer shows up at her door. He has brought Werner's recovered belongings with him, among them the little model of Etienne's house that Marie-Laure's father made. Jutta is able to track Marie-Laure down—at the museum where her father worked, and where she now works studying mollusks—and brings the house to her. Jutta also sends Frederick some pictures Werner ripped from Marie-Laure's book of birds, as Werner had wanted to do. The interconnectedness of these four people, all leading very different lives and generally oblivious to one another, is made palpable by Werner's presence in each their chapters.

This notion continues as the third epilogue, Part Thirteen, concludes the whole book in 2014. Marie-Laure walks with her grandson through the Jardin de Plantes; he's playing some game on a handheld device against another child somewhere else in the world, and the hollowness of the connection that technology offers becomes all too clear. But, Marie-Laure, wonders, with all the wires and fibers and transmitters and satellites, "is it so hard to believe that souls might also travel those paths?"

All the Light We Cannot See
A Sidekick to the Anthony Doerr Novel

Imagining Alternate Endings

I thought this novel ended exactly as it should have, striking just the right tone between harsh realism and cautious optimism. But still, it's hard not to dwell on Werner, and his choice to go in the opposite direction of Marie-Laure after getting her to safety. Couldn't he have kept up his disguise and stayed with her? It's nice to think of the kind of happily-ever-after love story ending that Werner's infatuation with Marie-Laure hints at. But more important than that, what if Werner was able to go free and have a second chance at life? To do right by Jutta and pursue things that made him feel complete? There would still be pieces to pick up, and the mental scars would last a lifetime. But it's nice to imagine Werner being given some kind of hope and the promise of a different, if not better, future.

Themes & Symbols You May Have Missed

20,000 Leagues Under the Sea

Jules Verne's book figures heavily throughout the novel: it acts as an anchor for Marie-Laure, a story in which she can lose herself, and she strongly identifies with its narrator, a French marine biologist named Professor Aronnax. What you might not have noticed, though, is that her great uncle Etienne shares many traits with Verne's antihero, Captain Nemo. Nemo was a scientific genius who developed and built his own submarine, the *Nautilus*. Etienne, too, had a knack for science, writing those scripts for the records he recorded with his brother, and building his own radio transmitter. Nemo lived almost his entire adult life in his submarine, shunning land-based society. After World War I, Etienne lived for twenty-four years in his house, never venturing out. Nemo cared deeply for members of his crew, and often blamed himself or felt guilt after a death. For Etienne, his brother's death was tremendously traumatic, and he felt guilty about it, even though he had nothing to do with it. The only time Nemo left his ship or helped outside parties was in the fight against what he saw as imperialist oppression.

Nemo often gave salvaged treasure and money to rebels or enemies of imperialistic states. Etienne finally emerges from his seclusion to take part in broadcasting codes for the French resistance, fighting Nazi imperialism.

Spirals

Spirals—in shape and concept—appear regularly throughout Doerr's novel. Nemo's ship, the *Nautilus*, is named for a type of sea shell with the spiral shape. Marie-Laure decides her undercover resistance name will be "The Whelk," another type of sea-snail with the spiral-shaped shell. A large spiral staircase goes up the center of Etienne's house. All of Marie-Laure's Jules Verne books are spiral bound. Frederick, severely brain-damaged from his beating at school, appears to do nothing more than draw spirals on sheets of paper all day long.

The spiral is a shape found throughout nature—not just in shells, but in the shape of our DNA, the shape of pine cones, the shape of our galaxy. There's a whole bunch of legitimate math that goes into the prevalence of this shape in nature, and if you're interested you should do a Google search on the Fibonacci Series or the Golden Ratio. Suffice it to say, there is something extraordinarily life-affirming about this set of geometric points, and Doerr sprinkles it throughout his novel. Consider, also, Werner's technique of triangulation, and think of how many perfect triangles you find in nature.

A Closer Look: Werner

In a review of *All the Light We Cannot See*, author William T. Vollman complained that Werner was not as completely realized a character as Marie-Laure. He wrote that Werner "lacked context" and grew to be "less knowable to us, less real." This is an unfair criticism of Werner, I think, in that Werner's lack of any kind of specific conviction apart from self-interest was his defining character trait, and it became the foundation of a wall he built around himself to shield the sensitive child within from the horrors he was participating in. As doubt crept into Werner's mind about the wisdom of his decision to get out of Children's House, he pushed the logical portion of that doubt away. Werner at school was a contrivance, but not one of Doerr's limited imagination. Rather, it was Doerr's talent that enabled him to create what I believe was a character realistically faking it.

In her Sidekick to *The Nightingale*, another tale set in WWII, Katherine R. Miller discusses the ambiguities inherent in Beck, a Nazi captain who, much like Werner, often remains unknowable to us, his actions and words at times in conflict and often open to different interpretations. Sometimes these characters who at first seem inconsistent or difficult to understand are worth a closer look, if not for the answers they give us, then for the questions they make us ask.

Consider Jutta, Werner's own sister, who arguably knew him better than anyone else apart from Frau Elena. Thirty-four years pass in between the time she last saw her brother and meeting Marie-Laure, and Jutta's gut instinct is to apologize to her for anything Werner might have done. She assumes he was just another Nazi monster. No one really knew Werner at that point of his life. Volkheimer, with his clear affection for Werner, came closest to knowing his inner torment, but that happened a day or two before they never saw each other again. It took that long for Werner to say anything personal. Yet Marie-Laure, for all of the twenty-four hours she knew him, may have known him best, as he finally allowed his true self—kind, moral, loving, sensitive—to be seen by her, and only her.

All the Light We Cannot See
A Sidekick to the Anthony Doerr Novel

If You Loved This Novel...

About Grace, by Anthony Doerr

Doerr's debut novel, *About Grace* concerns a hydrologist named David Winkler who begins dreaming about things that soon become true. Here, mysteries are found within snowflakes and their own magical world of geometric shapes as Doerr explores families, family relationships, and the lack of boundaries between the human and natural worlds (which are actually the same thing).

Slaughterhouse Five, by Kurt Vonnegut

Not just another postmodern novel about World War II (and the destruction of an ancient city), this may be *the* postmodern novel about World War II. Vonnegut's masterpiece frequently uses short, declarative sentences, and the book moves along at an odd rhythm. The absolutely magically absurd things described within its pages "are all true, more or less," according to the author himself. Vonnegut was not the only veteran of World War II to get out alive yet forever scarred by the experience, nor was he the first to attempt to write about it. He was, arguably, the person most up for the job of capturing the horror and irrationality of war, and there's a reason why schools are still banning this book, forty-five years later: because it's the truth.

Possible Storylines for a Sequel

While the ending may not have provided as full a catharsis as we might have wanted, this is too fully realized a story to suggest a sequel. What would be interesting, though, would be a second look at this same story, but through two other characters' eyes. What if we were to revisit these events, but our French character was Mme. Manec and the German one was Volkheimer? Both of them have more feeling and soul than many supporting characters, and they hint at complex backgrounds. As the help, Mme. Manec cared for Etienne for practically his entire life. What did she have to give up for that? Why was she so devoted to him? Likewise, Volkheimer was the proverbial Aryan superman: big, strong, following orders without question, no matter how gruesome. But he, too, had a softer, even tender, side, and it was his time with Werner that brought that out in him. How does someone who revels in the sounds of classical music and cares for his friend and colleague the way Volkheimer does end up shooting resistance fighters' heads off and stealing clothes from prisoners?

In the Final Analysis...

The world had never seen anything like the second "Great War." They said that after the first one, and the experience was thought to be enough to sour any thoughts of another try. But it didn't happen that way. Instead, World War II claimed a total of sixty million dead over six years (including the victims of the Holocaust), and left many scratching their heads and pondering serious existential questions. Out of this relativistic moral atmosphere was born the postmodern era, which informed all manner of art, from literature to painting to cinema. In a world that made no sense, the logical move for artistic expression was to echo (and therefore criticize) this state of things.

It is only fitting, then, that Anthony Doerr should pull out all the postmodern stops in *All the Light We Cannot See*. Using many of the techniques of the form, techniques which are defined by their not being traditional, Doerr accomplishes two things. First, seventy years after WWII and the birth of postmodernism, his use of unconventional literary technique is, at this point, conventional. As readers, we're no longer perplexed by Doerr's fractured chronology or flights of verbalistic fancy, which makes it the perfect motif to readdress a topic touched on by so many others already. The second accomplishment is that, in using the postmodern playbook to address the chaos and terror of WWII—the very same playbook devised to make sense of the atrocities—Doerr has cast an unusual light on the events and people of the time. Werner's not a bad guy, as most Nazi characters tend to be, and so we get a very human picture of the enemy, and one of the more realistic and moving portrayals of the war and its effects.

So, What'd You Think?

Thanks for investing in this *Sidekick*. Now that you've read it, let us hear from you!

In just a sentence or two, please email founders@welovenovels.com your answer to one simple question:

What was your favorite (or least favorite) thing about this Sidekick?

We want to know what you think, so we can bring you more of what you love most, and fix what you don't like.

And if you would like a free copy of Katherine Miller's top-rated *Sidekick* to *Leaving Time,* Jodi Picoult's latest bestseller, we'd like to send it to you (a $4.99 value). All you have to do is add the words "**Yes, I Want My Bonus Sidekick**" to the email subject line, and you'll get instant access.

All the Light We Cannot See
A Sidekick to the Anthony Doerr Novel

About the Author of This Sidekick

Dave Eagle is a writer and photographer living in Vermont. His essays have appeared on TheAtlantic.com, as well as several other websites that aren't nearly as impressive. When not reading, or writing, or writing about reading, Dave spends his time raising his two children, which leaves little time for anything else—and that's just fine by him, if you want to know the truth.

Other Sidekicks from WeLoveNovels

Sidekick to The Nightingale

Sidekick to Wayward

Sidekick to Seveneves

Sidekick to Departure

Sidekick to Orphan Train

Sidekick to Papertowns

Sidekick to Gathering Prey

Sidekick to Pines

Sidekick to Memory Man

Sidekick to The Shadows

Sidekick to The Husband's Secret

Sidekick to A Spool of Blue Thread

Sidekick to The DUFF

Sidekick to Insurgent

Sidekick to Redeployment

Sidekick to The Girl on the Train

Sidekick to Still Alice

Sidekick to Captivated by You

Sidekick to Catching Fire

Sidekick to Mockingjay

Sidekick to Deadline

Sidekick to Big Little Lies

Sidekick to Gone Girl

We are so grateful to all who have taken a moment to leave a quick review of one of our Sidekicks on Amazon. Your thoughtfulness means a lot and helps us, and the rest of the world, know how we are doing and how we can improve. :)

Other Books by Anthony Doerr

About Grace

Memory Wall

The Shell Collector

Questions? Ideas? Comments?

Email **founders@welovenovels.com**.

We are listening!

CPSIA information can be obtained
at www.ICGtesting.com
Printed in the USA
LVOW04s0052120116
470125LV00031B/754/P